T0381974

First published in the United Kingdom by
HarperCollins *Children's Books* in 2024
HarperCollins *Children's Books* is a division of HarperCollins*Publishers* Ltd
1 London Bridge Street
London SE1 9GF

www.harpercollins.co.uk

HarperCollins*Publishers*
Macken House, 39/40 Mayor Street Upper,
Dublin 1, D01 C9W8, Ireland

5

ISBN 978-0-00-856124-6

Adam Stower asserts the moral right to be identified
as the author and illustrator of the work.

A CIP catalogue record for this title is available from the British Library.

Printed and bound in the UK using 100% renewable electricity
at CPI Group (UK) Ltd

MURRAY AND BUN!

MURRAY the VIKING

ADAM STOWER

HarperCollins *Children's Books*

In a little house in an ordinary town lives a wizard called Fumblethumb. Fumblethumb is a rubbish wizard. He is terrible at magic.

But this story isn't about Fumblethumb.

This story is about his cat, Murray, and the magic cat flap.

This is Murray.

He likes things neat and tidy.

He likes snoozing, napping and sleeping (but not necessarily in that order).

He loves his bed and his fluffy blanket, Pickles.

He likes peace and quiet and warm sunshine (preferably dappled)

and dreams of one day having a custard-yellow cardigan of his very own.

He loves buns most of all, especially
sticky ones with a cherry on top.

So you can imagine how he felt when Fumblethumb 'accidentally' turned his last and best bun into . . .

. . . a rabbit!

Meet Bun.

Bun is a very **bouncy** rabbit
with a cherry for a tail.

He is also quite sticky.

er...

Bun loves EVERYTHING!

Especially adventure...

because it is bound to
be fun and lovely!

Murray sleeps in a little bed by the back door of the kitchen where Fumblethumb works.

Every morning after elevenses, Murray steps through his cat flap to have a stretch in the garden, a wee, and a roll in the grass if he is feeling particularly sporty.

It was a good life.

. . . but **mostly**, it leads to . . .

Adventure!!

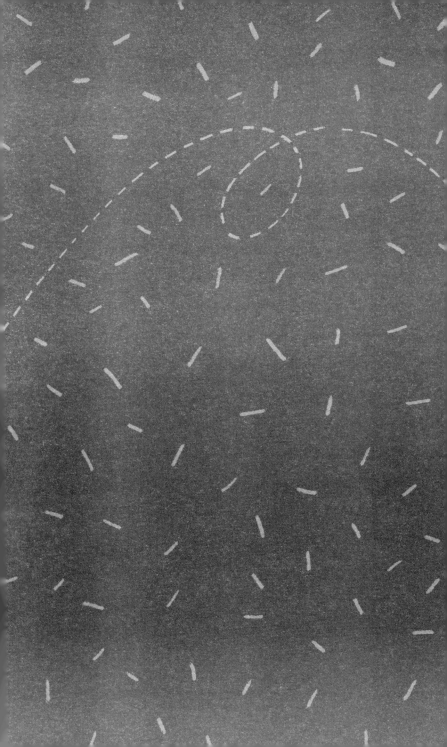

Murray opened one eye and looked at his cat flap suspiciously.

'It's looking awfully adventurous today, Bun.'

'BUN!' said Bun happily from above. He was stuck to the ceiling.

Again.

Murray suspected he ought to stay with his blanket, Pickles, where it was safe. But a loud POP had woken him up, and now Fumblethumb was running round the kitchen with his hat on fire, and the room was filling up with pink smoke.

Murray tried holding his breath, but it turned him blue and made his eyes bulge.

At this rate, he would have to go . . .
OUTSIDE! Murray coughed and
looked again at the back door.

'Oh, come on then, Bun,' he sighed, and he stepped gingerly through the flap.

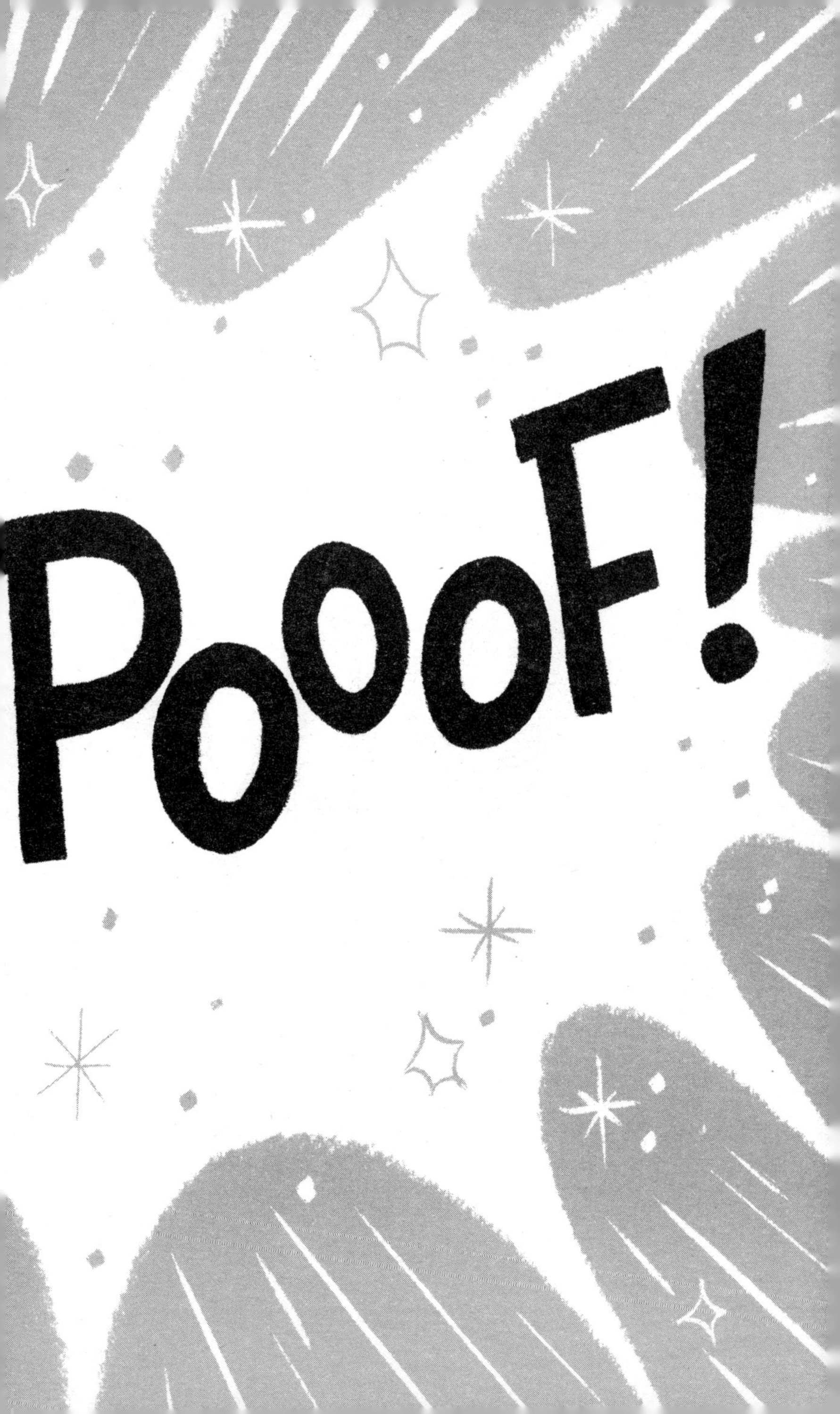
POOOF!

Murray and Bun found themselves in a large wooden hall packed full of hairy men and rosy-cheeked women. They all stared at Murray and Bun expectantly.

Murray hoped that any minute now someone would tell him where he was, what a 'troll' was, and how big you ought to be to hunt one.

Bun wasn't any help.

'I am Chief Harald the Hairy,' said an enormous beard with a man behind it.

Bun, who has very good manners, hugged the beard hello and got stuck.

The chief waggled a finger at Murray.

'Our friend Eggrik is MISSING!' he said.

'Gobbled up by TROLLS, I expect.'

Murray had a nasty feeling he was about to be told to do something adventurous.

'And find Eggrik!' he added as he plucked Bun from his beard and waved them off. 'Although I expect he's been gobbled up, like I said before.'

A big lady with strong arms and a cheeky smile picked up Murray and Bun and carried them out of the hall.

'You can't go TROLL HUNTING empty-handed,' she said.

'Come along to my hut and let's see what we can find.'

'I put plenty of logs on the fire. It will be ROARING by now,' she added as they pottered up the path to her hut.

Ooh, thought Murray hopefully. *Perhaps there will be sausages.* It had been minutes since breakfast, and he could feel a tummy rumble coming on.

But nothing in the hut looked very sausage-y at all.

Murray and Bun

Everything looked terribly adventurous, not very friendly and possibly even dangerous.

The shields were too BIG,

the hammers were too HEAVY,

44

and the armour PINCHED Murray in his plump parts.

Luckily, Murray's great-uncle Fergus was a blacksmith's cat, so Murray knew ALL about banging metal into useful shapes. Probably. He made himself something small enough to tuck inside his pocket.

Harald the Hairy stuck his big head in through the door.

'Come along! Come along!' he boomed. 'It's getting late! Time to go! Those trolls won't hunt themselves, y'know!'

He scooped up Murray and Bun and set them off on their adventure.

'The trolls are across the water in the Gobble-You-Up Woods on Troll Island,' said Chief Harald.

'Help yourself to a longship, and good luck!'

Murray and Bun followed the path to the water's edge and found a famous Viking longship.

They climbed aboard.

Luckily, Murray's great-great-grandpa, One-eyed-Jock, had been a ship's cat who sailed the high seas (and a few low ones) so Murray knew ALL about boats! Probably.

'The front end is this way,' he told Bun, tucking one hand in his belt and pointing importantly.

Bun was a curious rabbit and asked why Viking boats were called longships.

'Because they are . . . um . . . ships . . . and
. . . er . . . long,' said Murray, setting off along
the deck.

Bun was impressed.

And the ship was long too.

Very long.

Very . . . very long.

Much longer than you'd expect.

But surely the end was coming up soon?

Nope.

But like a true troll hunter, Murray carried on **valiantly.**

And by the time they reached the front, to sail to Troll Island . . .

Murray and Bun stood at the edge of
the Gobble-You-Up Woods and peered
into the shadows.

Something rustled in the trees.

Something was watching them.

(And it wasn't that squirrel.

Or that slug . . . or that pebble.)

Murray was just about to suggest perhaps having a little snack instead of hunting trolls . . .

. . . when Bun got all OVEREXCITED and charged ahead. As usual.

Murray didn't like the forest, and with every twig that poked him in his plump parts, and every muddy puddle that splashed his paws, he wished harder to be back at home with Pickles, where it was warm and safe and where there was probably a plate of fresh scones waiting for him too . . .

But Bun had vanished. He was LOST in Gobble-You-Up Woods!

So Murray searched
up every tree,

behind every boulder,

and under every slug,
until he found him . . .

. . . in a clearing . . .

. . . stuck to a . . .

Murray had never seen a troll before.

'I thought trolls would be bigger,' he said, suddenly feeling braver and plucking Bun from the tip of the troll's nose.

But then . . .

. . . Mummy Troll arrived . . .

and Daddy Troll too.

Suddenly, Murray didn't feel so brave after all.

And finally, along came . . .

. . . GRANDPA TROLL!

Bun said Grandpa Troll looked like a big walnut.

But it didn't help Murray feel better.

The trolls looked at Murray and Bun. They had a glint in their eyes. Murray knew that look all too well.

They were HUNGRY!

'It's time to eat a squidgy treat!' they said.

'OH NO!' shouted Murray, who was very fond of his plump parts.

'Oh dear!' said Mummy Troll. 'Don't you like picnics?'

'These herring sandwiches are delightfully squidgy!' said Daddy Troll.

HERRING SANDWICHES!

They were only Murray's third best
favourite treat ever!*

(*In his fish-snack category.)

There were few things in life that Murray liked better than picnics.

Troll hunting was turning out to be fun after all, thought Murray, as Daddy Troll poured everyone a cup of tea and Mummy Troll handed round the napkins.

'I like your green moustaches,' mumbled Murray through a mouthful of his fifth herring sandwich.

'Oh, these aren't moustaches,' said Grandpa
Troll, tugging something from his nostril.

'Do ALL trolls keep carrots up their noses?'
asked Murray. He liked learning new facts,
and he was trying hard not to notice Bun,
who was nibbling a carrot of his own, freshly
plucked from Grandpa Troll's other nostril.

'No, it's to block out the whiffy pong!'
said Grandpa Troll.

Murray had pretended not to notice, thinking it might have been the trolls, or Bun. But there was a whiff in the air.

Daddy Troll leaned closer. 'There is something in the woods,' he whispered. 'Something scary, hairy and very whiffy!'

'Oh dear,' said Murray. He gulped and asked the trolls if they knew anything about Eggrik. But the trolls just shrugged. They hadn't seen him.

Bun said that the Scary, Hairy, Whiffy Thing had got him, most likely.

The trolls all looked at Murray.

'Someone needs to go and investigate,' said Daddy Troll.

ahem...

Grandpa Troll gave Murray a herring for good luck, and they all waved goodbye as Murray and Bun strode heroically deeper into the woods.

'Adventuring always seems to be about DOING things rather than napping after eight herring sandwiches,' grumbled Murray as he and Bun searched for the Hairy, Scary, Whiffy Thing in the woods.

The only thing that could POSSIBLY make it worse would be a . . .

Bun said it wasn't that far to the other side. 'Just jump,' he said. 'You'll be fine,' he added. 'Probably.'

So Murray closed

his eyes . . .

. . . and jumped!

As it turned out, Bun was right. But Murray thought he didn't need to be so smug about it.

They followed their noses all the way to the bottom of a valley, where they found a hut . . .

. . . and crept gingerly inside.

Inside the hut, a large pot was bubbling over a fire. Something very gooey dripped from the ceiling and smelled so horrible it made Murray's eyes water.

Murray looked around, wishing he had brought his favourite pink rubber gloves with him. And a mop. He was very fond of tidiness.

. . . Something hairy, scary and VERY stinky burst through the door!

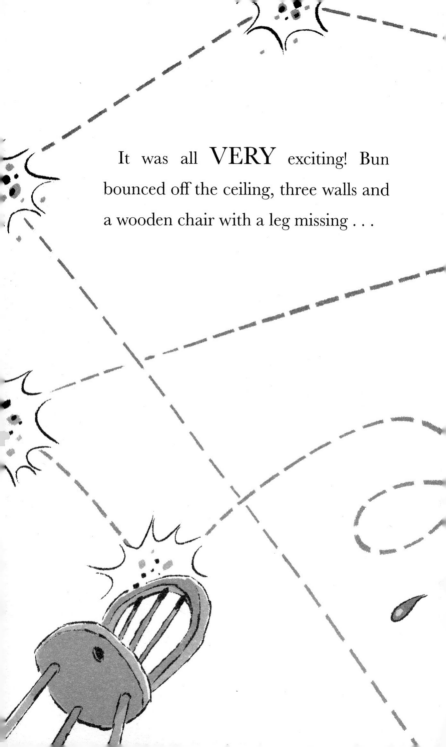

It was all VERY exciting! Bun bounced off the ceiling, three walls and a wooden chair with a leg missing . . .

. . . and ended up STUCK to the Thing's gooey belly!

Murray dashed to help. His BEST friend was in trouble. This was no time for naps. Not even snacks.

It was time for ACTION!

It was time for ADVENTURE!

He jumped at the Thing.

The Stinky Thing grabbed Murray with both arms and gripped him so tightly it made Murray's plump parts bulge.

Once the Thing had squeezed every last puff of breath out of Murray and Bun, it gently plonked them down and burst into tears.

'Um, hello,' said Murray, holding out a paw, 'I'm Murray. This is Bun. What kind of troll are you?' he asked politely, hoping it wasn't the kind that gobbled up Murrays or Buns.

'Not a troll!' the Thing said between sobs. 'I'm Eggrik!'

'Oh, hello, Eggrik! We've been looking for you.' Murray patted Eggrik's hand and wondered whether his lucky herring would help cheer him up.

'Eggrik . . . *sniff* . . . is LONELY!' Eggrik wailed.

'And HUNGRY . . . *sniff* . . . ' he went on.

Bun patted his other hand, and got stuck.

Murray stroked his whiskers thoughtfully. FOOD was his speciality. He cleared his throat importantly. He had an idea!

If he was hungry, Eggrik could make them all some tea. It was teatime after all, and it felt like ages since those eight herring sandwiches at the trolls' picnic. And if Eggrik was lonely, Murray and Bun would be his guests.

What an excellent idea! Murray plucked Bun from Eggrik's hand and they sat at the table. (Near the window. It was still very whiffy in the hut.)

Eggrik got busy.

He skipped around the kitchen laying the table with plates, knives, forks and hammers.

He fished around in the bubbling pot and plonked boiled eggs on each plate; one for Bun, three for Murray and seventeen for himself.

Murray was delighted. Boiled eggs were his third-favourite snack.*

(*In his egg category.)

But before he could get started . . .

. . . Eggrik burst into tears.

Again.

Wahh! Eggs all gone!

Runny egg dripped from the ceiling and dribbled down the walls. No wonder everything was SO whiffy!

Bun stuck himself to Eggrik again and patted him some more.

Murray didn't notice. It was hard for him to concentrate if there was a dippy egg nearby and his tummy was rumbling louder than ever.

He looked at the knife, fork and hammer,

then reached into his pocket . . .

. . . and fetched out
the little something
he had made earlier.

It worked
perfectly.

Eggrik was AMAZED! He had never seen a spoon before.

Murray looked at Eggrik's giant hammer and sucked the egg from his lucky herring thoughtfully.

'I think I know where you have been going wrong,' he said importantly.

Luckily, Murray's great-auntie Agatha was a teacher's cat, so Murray knew ALL about teaching. Probably. He gave Eggrik his little spoon . . .

Eggrik was soon full-to-bursting with lovely eggs and very happy.

It was time to go back to the village, announced Murray.

But Eggrik shook his hairy head sadly. All his dreams of building a chicken farm in the woods and having HUNDREDS of eggs had gone wrong. He missed the village, but now he was far too eggy and far too smelly to go home. Not even the trolls could stand his whiffy pong.

Murray stroked his whiskers. Eggrik was whiffy and he was pongy.

Murray had **another** idea!

He wrote a message and sent it to Chief Harald, via Eggrik's best messenger chicken.

Then they packed up all Eggrik's eggs, and his new spoon, and set off for the village.

They walked back through the woods . . .

. . . and hopped aboard the ship that Murray's message had asked the chief to send.

oof!

Eggrik was very excited!

He ran along the ship and . . .

. . . fell straight into the sea.

Murray and Bun fished Eggrik out of the water. He was as clean as a whistle! The Whiff had gone!

And together they sailed the SHORT ship back to the village.

Chief Harald and the Vikings welcomed them home.

'HOORAY! Eggrik is back!' boomed the

chief happily.

Three cheers
for the mighty
Troll Hunters!

Murray blushed. Bun did eight somersaults.

Chief Harald led Murray and Bun back to his big hut where a party was ready to begin.

'There's cake and jam and lemonade and as MUCH FISH AS YOU CAN EAT!' he said.

'It's just through this door. After you.'

Murray loosened his belt, ready for the feast (his trousers had been pinching his plump parts).

Bun hoped there would be dancing.

They skipped through the door . . .

. . . and found themselves back in Fumblethumb's kitchen.

'Oh, hello, you two! You're just in time for tea!' said Fumblethumb from behind a cloud of *green* smoke.

'You must be starving,' he said, plonking
Murray's dish on the floor.

The smoke cleared.

'Oh, brilliant,' sighed Murray.

THE END

How to draw Murray

1

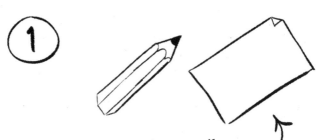

Get your favourite pencil and some paper.

2

First draw a slightly squashed circle for Murray's head.

Tip: If you use small scratchy lines, it will make it look furry.

Now add Murray's face.
This bit is tricky, so take your time.
He has **BIG** eyes and a small mouth.

Murray has a little body.

5

little
legs

Next add Murray's arms, legs and tail.

6

Now just pop on his ears
and whiskers.

(7)

Leave his face,
paws and tummy
white.

Don't forget
the shadow!

Lastly add shading for his fur.

Tip: Try using the edge of your pencil for this bit.

(8)

If you want to draw Murray dressed as a VIKING,
add his helmet, armour and cloak.

HOW TO
DRAW
A BUN

(1) (2)   (3)

What's that on Fumblethumb's mat?

POST CARD

Dear Fumbly,

When will you fix the catflap? Look where I am now! There are **Trolls*** here! If I get eaten I'll be very cross! For a bit anyway.

BUN says they will be lovely and there will be SNACKS, but you know what BUN is like.

Love Murray & BUN xxx

* not sure what 'TROLLS' are. But I feel wobbly...

TO:
FUMBLETHUMB the Wizard
The little house at the end.
No, not that one.
The one with the Yellow door.
That's the one.
ENGLAND

Great-great-Grandpa 'One-eyed JOCK'
— ship's cat —

Jock is 107 years old (in dog years) and won a ship of his own in a fierce game of 'SNAP' with PurpleBeard the Pirate. The ship is called The Naughty Susan and is feared by all who sail the seven seas.

Great Auntie AGATHA →

— Teacher's Cat —

The Cat sat on the mat
(and on the teacher's head when she was sleeping)

Great Uncle Fergus

— Blacksmith's Cat —

Fergus sat by the Forge and singed his tail so many times he was nicknamed 'Sizzle'

NEXT...

Dear Diary.

A big day! Today the **TRoll** Hunters arrived. I thought they would be bigger. And not <u>so</u> furry. Or sticky.

Still, I suppose the Chief knows what he's doing. I hope they find **Eggrik!** (He still owes me eight cabbages.)

I spilled more lunch down my best tunic today!!

It's hard eating Soup with a Hammer! (There <u>must</u> be an easier way?!) ♡

P.S. Tomorrow I'm going to pick some flowers for Big Hilda! ♡ ♡ ♡ ♡ ♡ ♡

MURRAY'S TOP 10

(1) Herring Sandwiches*
(* also number 3 in his
favourite fish-snack category)

(2) RHUBARB SNAPS

(3) Pickled Biscuits

(4) Mackerel Bonbons

(5) Those tiny sausages
on little sticks

Picnic Category

(6) Haddock Jellies

(7) PLUMP plum dumplings

(8) Ham 'n' Jam Sandwiches

(9) Broccoli Lollies

(10) Big Cake

BUN!*

* Bun loves them all of course.